A Home for Bilby

Joanne Crawford

Illustrated by

Grace Fielding

MAGABALA BOOKS

First published in 2004, reprinted 2005, 2006
Magabala Books Aboriginal Corporation, Broome, Western Australia
Website: www.magabala.com   Email: orders@magabala.com

Magabala Books receives financial assistance from the Commonwealth Government through the Australia
Council, its arts advisory body. The State of Western Australia has made an investment in this project through
ArtsWA in association with Lotterywest.

Designed by Pigs Might Fly Productions
Typeset in 14.5 pt Berkeley Book
Printed by Hyde Park Press, Adelaide

National Library of Australia
Cataloguing-in-Publication data:

Crawford, Joanne, 1963- .
A home for bilby.

For children.
ISBN 1 875641 91 2.

I. Fielding, Grace, 1948- . II. Title.

A823.4

About the Bilby

The bilby is a small, nocturnal Australian marsupial with blue–grey silky fur. It is a member of the bandicoot family and is sometimes known as the 'Greater Bilby'.

Many years ago the bilby was found in habitats throughout Australia. Loss of habitat and the threat of introduced animals such as cattle, foxes and feral cats has resulted in a significant decline in the bilby population and where it is to be found. The bilby is considered to be an endangered species and is now found mainly in Australia's central desert regions.

The word 'bilby' comes from the Yuwaalaraay language, an Aboriginal language from northern New South Wales.

There are many conservation groups who are working to save the bilby through breeding programs and increasing public awareness about its plight. If you would like more information, contact the 'Save the Bilby Fund' at the Queensland Parks and Wildlife Service ph: (07) 4654 1255 or visit the website www.easterbilby.com.au

It was a sunny day in the Australian bush and a happy place indeed for the many animals that lived there.

There was a lot of activity and the animals were playing and having fun.

Koala was still sleepy because he had just woken up from a nap. Kangaroo was having a drink from the stream where Platypus was swimming and splashing around.

Emu was talking to Wombat about something exciting that had happened to her that day. They were all very busy.

No-one saw the little animal
sitting alone under a small tree.
He sat there quietly watching
the other animals play and
run around.

The little animal had a long,
black tail with a white tip.
His fur was mostly bluish–grey
and he had a white belly.

But it was his ears that stood
out the most. They were rather
long and looked a little bit like
rabbits' ears.

Suddenly the laughter and noise stopped. The other animals had noticed the little creature and wandered over to where he sat under the tree.

'Who are you?' said Kangaroo. 'What are you doing here in our bush?'

The little animal was frightened but answered in a soft voice, 'My name is Bilby.'

'Bilby!' exclaimed the other animals.

'Why have you come here?' Platypus asked anxiously.

'I'm looking for a home', said Bilby. 'I usually sleep during the day but I haven't got many family left now so I need to find somewhere to live.'

'Well, I live on the plains. It's where I hop and jump around,' Kangaroo said rather impatiently. 'It suits me because I have very strong legs and I need lots of room to go about my business.'

He pointed towards the plains and said, 'That's my home and it's no place for a bilby.'

'My home is along that fence,' said Emu, pointing her leg. 'I run very fast and I need to stretch my long legs so the fence line is the place for me. Sometimes I run with the other emus and we don't always see small animals in our way.'

In a very huffy manner she added, 'You can see it's no place for a bilby.'

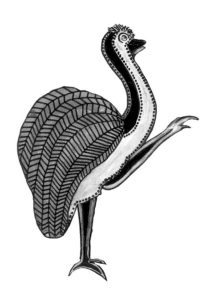

Koala looked at Bilby with a sympathetic look in his eyes. 'You see that gum tree with all the leaves on it? I live there,' he said, pointing at the tree.

'I eat the eucalyptus leaves and it is a safe home for me. But it's no place for a bilby,' he said sadly.

Wombat stood up and pointed to his burrow at the base of a large tree. 'That's my home,' he said. 'It's where I go and spend time by myself.'

As he ambled towards his burrow, he called out in a gruff voice, 'And I'm telling you now, it's no place for a bilby!'

Finally Platypus said, 'I live in the stream. It's a cool place where I swim and build nests from weeds and sticks with my long, flat, beak-like nose.'

With a flap of his tail, he looked at Bilby and said, 'I already share my stream with fish so it's no place for a bilby.'

After listening to the animals, Bilby hung his head and began to move away. A small tear ran down his cheek and his long ears hung down in a rather sad way.

The other animals huddled around. They felt sorry for the little bilby and after a short talk came up with an idea.

'Wait!' yelled Koala. 'We may have a home for you after all, if you're interested.'

Bilby turned around. 'Where?' he asked excitedly. 'Where do you think I can make my home?'

Kangaroo pointed to a small shrub. 'Over there, behind that shrub,' he told Bilby.

Bilby went over to the shrub and pulled it aside. There before him lay a pile of dirt. With his claws, he began to dig and before long he had carved out a splendid burrow. He even found some insects and seeds to eat. It was perfect.

At last he had found a new home and new friends. Just the right place for a bilby!

JOANNE CRAWFORD was born in Geraldton and has lived in the Midwest region of Western Australia all her life. She is a primary school teacher and has spent many years developing resources designed to provide teachers and students with a better understanding of Aboriginal culture.

A Home for Bilby is her first picture book and was inspired by her own children's fascination with the Australian bush and the many animals that live there.

GRACE FIELDING was raised at the Wandering Mission near Perth. She is well-known for her fabric printing and unique style that combines traditional dot art with contemporary images. Grace lives in Broome and works as a screenprinter for an Aboriginal women's resource centre where her designs are highly sought after.

She has illustrated two other children's books, one of which, *Bip the Snapping Bungaroo*, won the Crichton Award for Illustration in 1991.